Big Mum Plum

Daniel Postgate

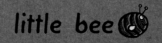

little bee

For Florence

First published in 2004 by Meadowside Children's Books
185 Fleet Street, London EC4A 2HS
This edition published in 2006 by Little Bee
An imprint of Meadowside Children's Books

Text and illustrations © Daniel Postgate 2004
The right of Daniel Postgate to be identified as the author
and illustrator has been asserted by him in accordance
with the Copyright, Designs and Patents Act, 1988

A CIP catalogue record for this book is available
from the British Library
10 9 8 7 6 5 4 3
Printed in China

"Now listen up," said Big Mum Plum,
"And hear the words I say -
Eat your porridge everyone...

...You're off to school today!"

That gave her pigs a mighty scare.

They jumped from table, stool and chair

And scattered here, there, everywhere

And hid themselves away.

"Oh, you can run,"
yelled Big Mum Plum.
"But I will always find you...
"You creep into that hiding place,
So very secret, very safe,
Then turn around, you'll see the face
Of BIG MUM PLUM behind you!"

The first to go was porky Paul,
Behind the coat-rack in the hall.
A clever place to hide, no doubt...

...Except his feet were sticking out.

Then after him was sneezy Tim,
Who hid inside the washing bin.
He nearly got away with it,

CHOO!

Until he had
a sneezing fit.

The next one out was Betsy-Mae.
Oh, what a place to hide away!
Big Mum Plum she
pulled the chain...

SLOSH

...Dear Betsy won't
hide there again.

Number four was sooty Sid.

Up the chimney Sid had hid.

Mum grabbed her brush and, pole-by-pole,

She shoved it up the darkened hole...

...Until she heard the pleasing 'POP',
Of Sidney coming out the top.

Out in the yard Mum spotted Lance,
Squatting by the potted plants.
She stalked him like a cunning fox...

...And caught
him by the hollyhocks.

Then into Suzie's room crept Mum
And blew on Sue's euphonium.
She blew it hard with depth and feeling.

PARP

Suzie nearly hit the ceiling!

And last of all, of course, was Trevor.
Trevor, being oh-so-clever,
Hid away in Big Mum's car,
The wisest place to hide by far.

How smart of you, dear Trev.
Well done...

...But not as smart as
BIG MUM PLUM!

Mum loaded all her pigs on board,
Then off to scary school they roared.

But when they got there,
What they saw,
Just wasn't scary, not at all...

Photographs of far-off places,
Painted plates with funny faces,
Tips on how to tie your laces,
Butterflies on strings.

And best of all was small Miss Peach,
Who welcomed them and made a speech,
On how much she would love to teach
Them lots and lots of things.

The pigs had such a smashing day,
They didn't want to go away,
They all decided they would stay
When home time came around.

Off they went - north, south, east, west -
Into cupboard,
trunk and chest.

Poor Miss Peach, she did her best
But not one pig she found.

Then through the door
Came Big Mum Plum
And with a roar
of **"Here I come!"**
She caught them all,
Yes, every one.

And when the dreadful
deed was done...

She took them home for
buttered bun
And chocolate spread
on toast.

"School is great! Yes, school is fun!
We love our school!" They told their mum.
"But not as much as
Big Mum Plum."